GOLDEN TURNABOUT

a story by **Michael Christopher**

D1253119

Golden Turnabout
Copyright © 2012, by Michael Christopher
All rights reserved
This book may not be copied or reprinted for
commercial gain or profit.
The use of short quotations or occasional page copying
for personal or group study is permitted.

Unless otherwise indicated, all Scripture quotations
are from *The Holy Bible,* King James Version (KJV)
The Holy Bible, New International Version (NIV)
© 1973, 1984 by International Bible Society,
used by permission of Zondervan Publishing House

Cover and interior design by garowski.com

This book made available without charge by The 1687
Foundation, a nonprofit, tax-exempt organization
dedicated to advancing spiritual and charitable
purposes. Please note that these books may only be
given away.
They cannot be sold, cannot be used to raise money,
and cannot be a "free giveaway" for any commercial or
personal-gain purpose whatsoever.

The 1687 Foundation First Printing, 2011
Printed in the United States of America
For additional information, please contact:

Email: info@1687foundation.com
Tel: 541.549.7600
Fax: 541.549.7603

So in everything, do to others what you would
have them do to you,
for this sums up the Law and the Prophets.
(Matthew 7:12, NIV)

Do not say,
"I'll do to them as they have done to me;
I'll pay them back for what they did."
(Proverbs 24:29, NIV)

Contents

A Word from Dellie

If you've never read a book called *Dellie O'Shea* you won't know much about me. So maybe I'd better introduce myself.

My birth name was Delbert Stevens but I've been called Dellie O'Shea most of my life. I was born in 1885. I grew up in Connecticut but I spent many years in Missouri. Plus a few other states along the way.

During much of that time I was a singer and a dancer, although I found myself in the middle of a lot of other adventures, too. Like robbery, kidnapping, and things even worse than that. But I was always on the right side of the law even though I sometimes had to dance pretty fast to stay there.

Two more things you ought to know. First, I wasn't much of a Christian during most of those adventures. But I should have been, because when the story I'm about to tell you popped back into my memory, many years after it happened, it made me remember once again that God had been watching out for me for a long time. He'd never stopped giving me lessons on what He was all about, even though I didn't always pay attention.

I'm hoping you will.

Finally, I really didn't want to mention this but somewhere along the line you've got to know it. I am what people used to call a "midget." Nowadays they'd call me a "little person," but to me it's all the same. At my very tallest I was never more than twenty-seven inches high, and never weighed more than sixty-five pounds.

I'm not sure that my size had anything to do with the way this story worked out, which happened about 1897 or so, when I was twelve years old. So I'll let you decide…

CHAPTER 1

Seth Farnum arrived just after lunch. We were working on our multiplication tables. I had barely finished reciting the fives and Paisley Baker was working on the sixes. Half an hour earlier she had given me a small slab of chocolate cake, which was just one of two good reasons why "Cake" was her official nickname.

She was about halfway through when we heard a knock on the door. Mrs. Frantom raised her hand for silence, then walked over and opened it up. In came the school principal, along with a nice-looking lady about the same age as my mother. And a new kid that we'd never seen before.

I don't remember anything unusual about him except for one thing. He kept looking out the window while the principal was talking, even when the whole conversation was focused on himself. And when they asked him one or two questions, which the rest of us couldn't really hear, his eyes went sideways even though he turned his head and aimed it at the adults. Plus, he didn't seem to be answering very well.

Sure enough, when his mother and the principal left, Mrs. Frantom sat the new guy down at the empty desk in front of me. "Class, we have a new student today. This is Seth Farnum. Let's make him feel welcome!"

Everybody banged their hands together right on cue while the new guy looked at the floor. Seconds before, when he walked by me he managed to look right through me as though I wasn't there. I knew right away we had a problem. Ten minutes later, after things quieted down and the arithmetic lesson had resumed, I tapped him on the shoulder so I could whisper something and found out things were a whole lot worse than I could have imagined.

Instantly his hand came slashing across his chest and grabbed my finger before I could jerk it back. He then slammed it down toward the floor, whipped his head around, and hissed at me like a snake.

"Don't touch me! Don't you touch me! You keep your hands off me!"

At least we now knew he could talk. But if we'd been outside, without a teacher watching, I think I would have shut him up pretty fast. As it was, Mrs. Frantom came hustling over but didn't really do anything. Just gave me a frosty-eyed look and then walked away.

At the end of the day she motioned for me to stay behind as the others scrambled for the door. "What happened, Dellie?" she said when the room had cleared. "What was that ruckus all about?"

"I don't really know, Mrs. Frantom. I touched him on the shoulder to see if he wanted to borrow a pencil—and maybe some paper. He didn't have anything like that with him, but I guess he didn't want any."

Mrs. Frantom appeared to be thinking hard before she answered. "Dellie, I knew Seth would be coming today, and I knew from talking to his mother last week that he might be a little touchy sometimes. I meant to say something to the whole class this morning, but I finally decided not to bring anything up if I didn't have to. Sometimes it's better not to invite trouble on purpose."

She motioned me into a chair beside her desk, then sat down behind it before she continued.

"Seth Farnum is a little bit different, Dellie. He's a fine young man and he's probably very smart, but he doesn't always relate to other people the way most of us do. We have to give him room and cut him slack until we can all figure out the best way to get along with him. In a way, maybe working with Seth could be a good lesson for all of us. You can't live very long without running up against people who react to things a little differently than others. What you thought of as a friendly gesture might have seemed like you were pushing your way into Seth's own space. Do you understand what I mean?"

I wasn't sure but I nodded anyway.

"Good. I can't be any more specific than that right now, but if you and the others in the class are willing to work a little harder to make friends with Seth, I think all of this will work itself out very quickly. You'll see—I'll bet he'll wind up being one of your best buddies before the year is over!"

I didn't think so but I knew enough not to argue.

A DECENT EXPLANATION

CHAPTER 2

The youth group that Cake Baker had got me involved in several months earlier was scheduled for our weekly meeting that evening. She came across the street to my house after supper and we walked over to Brian Morgan's place together.

"What did you do to Seth Farnum?" she said on the way. "Did you hit him or pull on his pants?"

"Neither one. I tapped him on the shoulder so I could loan him a pencil. Never saw anybody get so shook up over nothing!"

"Maybe he thought you were planting a cockroach on him. Wouldn't be the first time, would it?"

We both knew she was right so I didn't have much of an answer. By the time we got to Brian's house his dad was standing on the porch, welcoming all of us as we arrived. In a matter of minutes more than a dozen kids were inside, sitting in a circle and eating cookies passed out by Brian's mother.

"So," Mr. Morgan finally said, nodding at the group. "Let's begin with prayer and then we'll get into tonight's topic." He closed his eyes, asked God to bless all of us, and then pulled out a huge Bible that must have weighed about ten pounds.

"I want to read just one verse tonight, from the gospel of Matthew. Chapter 7, verse 12, for those who want to follow along: 'Therefore all things whatsoever ye would that men should do to you, do ye even so to them.'"

As always, Mr. Morgan read from the *King James Version* of the Bible, which was just about the only one we had available back in the last few years of the nineteenth century. Most of the modern translations hadn't come out yet, so we were still dealing with seventeenth century English. And it wasn't always so easy to figure out. Which is why Mr. Morgan's next comment was so predictable.

"All right," he said. "This is a quotation direct from Christ Himself. Who can put it into modern English? Into simple language we can all understand? What was He saying?"

Immediately a half-dozen hands shot up.

"Okay, Henry, I think you were first. What do you think?"

Henry Vanderpool—most of us called him Hank—was the tallest kid in the room. Eventually he would grow to be well over six feet, which was pretty tall for that era. But he wasn't exactly graceful at that age, and this time he'd shot his hand up so fast he almost tipped over his chair. But he recovered almost as fast.

"Isn't this what they call the golden rule?" he said. "Isn't this the one that means we should treat others the way we'd like them to treat us?"

"Could be," said Mr. Morgan. "Anybody else have an opinion?"

At that point he called on three more kids, all of whom said almost the same thing Hank had said.

"Okay," Mr. Morgan responded at last. "It looks like we all agree with each other. But"—and here he scratched his face two or three times as though he was thinking really hard—"what does this mean in real life? What does it mean in *your* life? Can anybody give me a real example?"

More hands shot up immediately, and Mr. Morgan went around the room quickly, pointing at each hand-raiser in turn until we'd heard from almost everybody.

"It means not beating up on your brothers or your sisters."

"It means not cheating on a test by looking at someone else's paper."

"It means not lying to your parents so they won't lie to you."

"It means following the rules when you play a game, so the others won't feel like they have a right to cheat, too."

"It means doing a good job when you work for somebody else, so they'll know you've actually earned whatever they pay you."

"It means being as valuable to the rest of the world as you can be—like gold. It also means not rotting, or rusting, or being too set in your ways to adapt yourself to the situation and fit in. As long as you don't give up your identity in Christ."

That one came from Mrs. Morgan herself—the one who usually baked the cookies and kept quiet. For once I guess she just couldn't help jumping in. But the last hand belonged to Cake Baker, who changed the game instantly.

"It means being patient with someone who might seem a little weird—someone who's new to your class, whose eyes go sideways a lot like he can't look you in the face. Someone who also doesn't act like he really wants to talk to you."

Every kid in that room knew instantly that Cake Baker was talking about Seth Farnum. And even though I expected that Mr. Morgan would have no idea who the object of her comment might have been, he didn't seem the least bit surprised.

"You want to tell us about it, Paisley?" As with Hank, he was one of the few—even among the adults—who almost never used Paisley Baker's nickname.

She seemed a little hesitant at first, like she might have said more than she intended to, but she couldn't back down now. "His name is Seth," she finally said, fumbling a little bit with the words. "In some ways he seems like a perfectly normal kid, but he's only been in our class one day and already he's blown up at Dellie. And he won't look at any of us, or talk normal to us either. And yet I know we've got to treat him like we'd want him to treat us or we'll just make things worse."

One or two of the other kids in the room nodded their heads. But Mr. Morgan bowed his instead, as though he couldn't think of anything to say. Finally, after a long silence he shook it back and forth, very gently, before he began to talk again.

"Listen, everyone," he began, very slowly and very quietly. "I know exactly who you're talking about and I know exactly what you mean. I also know that Seth Farnum can seem a little distant and a little hard to take sometimes. But here's the thing you need to understand. I've had two or three long conversations with both of Seth's parents. They're pretty new in town but they've been here more than a month and they've just now made the decision to put Seth in school with all of you rather than teaching him at home. Seth is actually a very intelligent young man, but he definitely has some social problems that keep him from fitting in with everyone else, in ways that his parents—and you folks as well—might want him to."

He hesitated for a moment, as though he was either trying to think of what to say next or waiting for questions from the group. But nobody said a word and eventually Mr. Morgan continued.

"My understanding of the condition Seth has is that it's not a real disease—it's simply a reflection of how his brain seems to work. But it can also become physical, too, in ways that don't always make sense. However, you have to understand that it's not Seth's fault. Not all of us are put together in exactly the same way. To repeat what I just said, in Seth's case it's simply the way his brain works. Mostly, he doesn't know how to relate to other people on a regular basis, like the rest of you do. So he pulls back, sometimes seems like he's ready to fight, and hardly ever seems to fit into a group like he probably wishes he could."

"I don't understand," said Cake. "Why haven't we heard about this kind of thing before? Why haven't we seen any other cases?"

"Like I said," Mr. Morgan responded, "It's a minor condition in which someone's brain doesn't always work exactly like everyone else's. It's actually been around for a long time, but most people don't know much about it because it's pretty rare. And, the doctors don't yet understood it well enough to give it a name and start sharing information about it. That will happen eventually, I'm sure, but it hasn't happened yet.

"At this point, Seth Farnum has been diagnosed by some pretty good doctors, and I've been shown most of their opinions, on paper, so that I could help advise his parents. I want you to know that I told them you'd be the best possible group for him to join. That you'd all make a huge effort to understand him, to not judge him, and to get along with him without any trouble."

Mr. Morgan stopped for a moment and looked slowly around the room, at each of us in turn. Then he seemed to get even more serious.

"The only thing we weren't sure of was whether we should tell the whole class in advance. Obviously, I'm telling you folks now because you're already asking questions and you deserve to have some answers. And, because I know your hearts and I know you'll treat him with love, charity, and lots of understanding—exactly as you'd like to be treated if you were in his shoes."

One of the guys turned his head so that Mr. Morgan couldn't see him roll his eyes. Beyond that, I don't think anyone said a word for at least a full minute. Once again Mr. Morgan continued.

"The other side of the coin can be a little more positive. Many times people with a condition like this have what we medical folks call 'compensatory abilities.' That means they can sometimes do other things better than the rest of us. No one really knows why, and Seth is still quite young, so his parents haven't really identified any for sure. Except for one thing. He does seem to have an unusual ability to work with animals. They tell me it's almost as though he can speak their language—like he knows what they're thinking. Now maybe that's true and maybe it's not, but either way he's definitely a good kid on the inside. He's not mean and he's not a fighter, except that he sometimes overreacts to things when he doesn't instantly recognize what's going on around him."

At that point Eric Topper raised his hand and made a typical suggestion, for him. "Why don't we invite him to our picnic next weekend? Let's get to know him and give him a chance to know us."

Heads were beginning to nod all over the room, some faster than others. Mr. Morgan's was probably the last one to start moving. "Good. Good idea," he said. "Let's do that! Dellie, why don't you ask him for us when you see him at school tomorrow?"

I wasn't sure I wanted to, especially after the way Seth had reacted to me earlier that same day. But I also knew that if I invited him to a picnic he couldn't possibly think of that as an insult and get mad again. Plus, it might help smooth things over.

So I agreed.

CHAPTER 3

When I got to school the next morning Seth Farnum was already there. He was sitting just ahead of my own desk with his head buried in a book, like he'd come a little more prepared than he had been before.

"What'cha reading," I asked, dumping down my own books with a huge thump. He turned halfway around and for the first time looked right at me.

"Nothing much," he said, by which time his eyes had gone sideways again. "Catching up on some arithmetic stuff." His voice seemed a little odd, like he couldn't get all the sounds out clearly. He seemed to be speaking out of the side of his mouth, like maybe he couldn't quite arrange his lips straight.

"Look, I hope you understand that I wasn't trying to bug you yesterday. I just wanted to offer you some paper and a pencil. I didn't mean to startle you."

"Okay. I get scared. Don't like people's hands on me."

"Fair enough," I said, turning away to arrange the books and papers on my own desk. "Actually, I don't either! Oh—and one more thing I wanted to ask. We have a youth group that meets once a week and talks about things. Mostly Bible things, like how to be better people. We're having a picnic at one of our parents' place next weekend. Saturday, around 11 o'clock in the morning. Any chance you might be able to come? We might have horses to ride, and we'd be glad to have you."

He looked pained again, and then he suddenly smiled in a distorted, grimacing sort of way. He definitely had some mouth control issues! He also seemed almost overwhelmed at the thought, and stuttered several times before he finally got a few words out.

"Hav-hav-have to ask mom. Have to ask. Tell you tomorrow. Tomorrow."

True to his word, Seth had an answer for me next morning, which he delivered the minute he saw me with no preliminaries at all.

"She said I can go!" he said. "She said I can go! But she said to ask you where, so I'd know how to get there. Is it close enough to walk?"

At that point I asked Seth where he lived. Turns out it was only two streets over from my place, in a house with a huge yard that I knew had been vacant for several months. So I made the obvious suggestion.

"Why don't you walk over with Cake Baker and me? It's only a few blocks, right on the edge of town. It'll take us about twenty minutes. We could stop by your place about 10:30 or so and go from there."

Again he hesitated, this time for almost a full minute. "I guess that would be all right," he finally said. "But I'm not really a fast walker."

I couldn't help smiling, given how much shorter my legs were than his. Normally I never made any kind of references to my size, but this was an obvious exception. I pointed down toward my feet.

"I'm the one who usually has to run to keep up," I said. I don't think 'slow walking' will be a problem."

Later that day, when I told Cake Baker that we'd be stopping at Seth Farnum's house on the way over to Joey Falcon's, she wasn't too happy. "I don't know what it is about him, but I don't think very many people are comfortable with him at this point. I understand what Mr. Morgan said, but the guy is still a little bit weird. And that's hard to like."

I let it go because I knew she was right.

CHAPTER 4

On Saturday morning, right on schedule, Cake and I walked over to Seth Farnum's place and knocked on the door. Nothing happened for a long time, so we knocked again. Eventually we heard footsteps from inside, and finally Seth opened the door.

"I'll be ready in a minute," he said. "But my mother wants to ask you something first."

At that point the same woman who had brought him to school that first day stuck her head out the door and looked us over carefully. "Is this a church group?" she said, with a really strange look on her face. She didn't seem to like the idea.

"Yes it is," said Cake. "But it's not about church stuff today, Mrs. Farnum. It's a picnic at Joey Falcon's place, with maybe some games of some kind. Mostly fun stuff, like a party."

Apparently that satisfied Seth's mother, because she nodded her head and backed up a little bit. Immediately Seth pushed his way past her and started walking down the path beside the road. Fortunately he headed off in the right direction.

The rest of the trip over to Joey's house went fairly smooth, without any major hitches. But it also didn't include much talking. Cake and I both tried two or three times to get something going, but Seth kept giving us one-word answers until we both shut up.

Once we arrived we sort of melted into the crowd and Seth was on his own. Once again he seemed like he was in the wrong place, until he suddenly pointed toward the pasture just beyond the fence around the backyard, where Joey's father kept two of their horses.

"Hey!" he said. "Ride one?"

Joey Falcon laughed, and shook his head. "Yeah, you could ride them if you could catch them. They've both been trained. But most of the time, neither one will come when you want him to. You'd have to figure out how to get 'em up here where we can saddle 'em!"

Seth lowered his head and acted like he was thinking, and said something so quietly that none of us really heard it.

"What?" said Joey. "I couldn't tell what you said."

Seth spoke up a little bit. "I said I could catch one. Not a problem. You give me a piece of rope, I'll get one for you."

It wasn't hard to tell that Joey wasn't impressed. He made a horrible face—sort of a combination between a frown and a smile, like he couldn't decide which one. Finally he got it under control.

"I can get you the rope, but you gotta' promise me you won't get hurt. The black one is called Thunder and the other one is called Lightning. She's the reddish-brown one, which is what we call a 'bay.' They're both good horses but you can't be chasing 'em around 'cause you'll never get near 'em, if that's what you have in mind. And if you press them too hard they might run right over you."

"No—no. No problem! Just give me rope—give me rope! Give me rope and I'll show you how to catch."

By that time, Seth and Joey had the full attention of the whole crowd, including Joey's father who had been busy building a fire to cook with. I think Joey still wasn't convinced, but he shrugged his shoulders and disappeared into one of the small sheds nearby. When he came out he had a coil of rope in one hand and a halter in the other. For a minute I thought his dad was going to step in and stop whatever was about to happen. Instead he looked right at Seth and added his own warning.

"You be careful, son," he said. "Those aren't mean horses or I wouldn't let you go out there at all. If you can get a rope on one of their necks he'll come right in. But like Joey said, don't be trying to chase them around 'cause they won't like that! And don't go throwing a lasso at them, either. You understand?"

Seth nodded his head, took the rope from Joey, and slowly folded it into his left hand with maybe a foot hanging out. Not coiled, mind you, but folded—which Joey somehow seemed to understand, judging by the surprised look on his face. I learned later on that Seth was simply using good horse sense. If you fold the rope you can let it go all at once if the horse panics and pulls away so hard you can't hold him. If you coil the rope around your hand it can get caught and your arm can get jerked right out of its socket. Or broken.

Seth must have known all that but I can't imagine how. Anyway, once he was ready he climbed over the fence. I don't know why he didn't use the gate, and I'm not sure that Joey's dad was too happy with the way he pulled on the wires. But at least there weren't any barbs on the top to catch his clothes or cut his fingers. That's another thing I learned later. You don't put barbed wire next to a horse. If there's a single sharp point on a hundred yards of fence they'll find it and cut themselves.

By the time Seth had landed on the other side, the black horse had turned to look straight at him. The bay horse was way off to the side, looking the other way, but the one they called Thunder was all eyes and ears. Until that point he'd been munching on the grass, but suddenly Seth had his full attention. I think that's what Seth wanted all along. He never hesitated; he just started walking straight at the horse, with no holding back whatsoever.

I would guess that Thunder was probably a good thirty to forty yards away when all this started. Quite a distance, in fact—it was a pretty big pasture, and there was still quite a bunch of room behind him, too. So not much happened right away.

However, once Seth had moved maybe twenty or thirty feet, with Thunder looking at him all the way, the horse suddenly tossed his head and backed up. Instantly, Seth stopped and slowly backed up too, three or four short steps. Then he stopped, and after a minute or so, Thunder began to move forward and Seth did the same.

Once more Thunder stopped and then backed up again. And once more, Seth did the same thing. Then they both did it again. And again. And once again. In fact, the whole sequence got repeated over and over, about a dozen times. And somewhere along the line the rest of us caught on to what was going on. Every time Seth and the horse matched each other's movements Seth gained another six or seven feet, and all of a sudden he found himself standing right beside the horse.

He then reached out with his free hand, patted the horse on the neck, and stroked him down across the withers for two or three minutes, all the while appearing to talk to him very quietly. Then he slipped the end of the rope around Thunder's neck and held it tight with his right hand, just behind the horse's ears, with the rest of it still folded in his other hand. At that point he had enough leverage to move the horse's head, and he began to lead him back toward the crowd. By that time we were all holding our breath, which we kept on doing until Seth brought the horse all the way to the fence next to us, slipped on the halter Joey handed him, and tied him up.

"Here's one of them," he said to Joey and his father, who had both dropped what they were doing to watch the whole process with their mouths hanging open.

"Well I never . . . " the father said at last. "I don't think I ever saw anything like that!"

"Just have to move toward him when he says it's okay. Not before. And back up to make him curious so he'll give you another chance."

In all the years that have passed since that day, I have never understood how Seth Farnum learned all that about horses. But somehow he knew. He also understood it well enough to explain it in a way that made perfect sense . . . or so I thought at the time. Joey's dad must have felt the same way too, because he just shook his head and grinned.

Eventually Joey got his mouth closed again, at which point he walked back into the same shed he'd got the rope from and brought out a saddle, plus the leather reins and the other parts that go over the horse's head. Taken together they call all of this stuff "tack," but I didn't really know that at the time. It was all a hodgepodge to me.

Now it was Joey's turn to show that he also knew what he was doing. Within a few minutes he had Thunder, the curious horse that nobody but Seth Farnum could catch, all saddled up and ready to ride.

CHAPTER 5

For the next hour or so, seven or eight kids climbed up on Thunder's back, one at a time, and rode him around in a circle maybe a hundred feet wide, usually with Joey Falcon leading him on a rope. Most of them seemed to know a little bit about riding, which made sense when you remember that we didn't have many other kinds of transportation in that era. No one fell off, and nobody looked like he was hanging on for dear life.

Strangely enough, Seth wasn't the first one to ride Thunder. Once they had him saddled he seemed to hold back. In the meantime he did the same crazy advance-and-retreat dance again and wound up catching and bringing in the other horse, too, the one they called Lightning. Then, after they put a halter on that one and tied her to the fence, when the next kid came back and dismounted Seth finally got on Thunder himself.

It didn't take him more than a few seconds to turn Thunder toward the open grass and urge him into a gallop. He ran him all the way to the farthest fence, way down the line, then turned him around and started galloping back. About halfway he slowed the horse to a walk and let him amble back to where the rest of us were watching. Thunder hadn't even broken a sweat yet.

At that point it was my turn. This wasn't the first time I'd ever been on a horse, but I had a huge disadvantage the other kids didn't have to deal with. I was so much shorter, with legs that were only about half as long as theirs were. Joey Falcon had to shorten the stirrups to the very last buckle. And even that wasn't quite enough. He finally took two rags and wrapped one around the bottom rung of each stirrup. That shortened the distance just enough so I could slip my foot in and balance myself in the stirrups. But just barely. And then it happened.

One of the kids had a sheet of white paper that he was scribbling something on. I guess one of the others tried to take it away so they could see what he was writing, and pretty soon the two guys were pushing each other back and forth while the first kid held the paper high above his head, laughing like a lamebrain.

Meanwhile, Thunder began flopping his head back and forth, trying to see what the commotion was all about. And I was trying to talk to the other kids and get them all to calm down, because I could see that Thunder was getting more and more nervous.

I'm not sure what happened next, but somehow I think the kid with the paper got shoved up against the fence, which made him let it go. Immediately the breeze caught it and blew it up against Thunder's head. And that's all it took.

Now, I know you're not supposed to swing up on a horse without having the reins in your hand already. But I wasn't able to get on that way. If I'd been by myself I'd have used a box to stand on, but given the way we were all sort of "helping each other out," two or three of the guys had hoisted me up while another one held the reins. At that point they'd fussed with my feet and tried to adjust the stirrups, as I said before.

Unfortunately, all of this business with the blowing paper happened at almost exactly the moment when I got both feet into the rag-padded stirrups. As my father used to say, thank heaven for small favors. Without those stirrups I never would have hung on through what happened next.

Thunder reared up on his hind legs, pulled the reins out of Joey Falcon's hands, banged his back end against the fence, and then took off running, full speed, as soon as his front hooves hit the ground again. And frankly, with the reins dancing along in front of him and whipping against his legs, I think they just made things worse. More important than that, without having them in my hands I had no hope of controlling him at all.

In fact, I was mighty lucky to grab his mane and hang on when he went up in the air. By the time he reached a full gallop I'd wrapped my arms around his neck as far as they'd go and squeezed him as tight as I could. In that position I was straddling the saddle horn with most of my weight on Thunder's neck. My feet were still in the stirrups, which were pushed forward as far as they'd go. And my head was turned sideways, to the left, tightly pressed down into his mane.

Even so I could see enough to know that we were heading straight for the fence at the far end of the pasture. I tried to push his neck sideways but it didn't help. Surely he'll turn, I thought. Sure he will! But he didn't.

I honestly don't know how I held on through that jump. Thunder sailed over the fence like a trained jumping horse, front legs folded up high and his head stretched straight out with his neck pretty much parallel to the ground. Again, I don't know how I held on, especially when we landed in a huge thump on the other side. But I did. My legs were absolutely rigid, pushing so hard against the stirrups I could feel my toes cramping up.

To make things worse, the smooth grass of the pasture ended at the fence. From there on it was all untamed country, with small bushes and a few scattered trees leading into a thick woods no more than two or three hundred yards away. We were headed straight for the forest, and if anything, Thunder seemed to be running faster all the time.

I remember praying as hard as I could that God would somehow work this out. I knew that I didn't dare let go and fall off. On this side of the fence there were rocks all over the place. All it would take would be one or two of those to bash me into a mush ball. On we went, for another hundred yards or so, with Thunder beginning to pant but not showing the least inclination to slow down. And certainly not to stop.

Suddenly, I thought I heard something else. It was hard to tell the difference, but it seemed like I was hearing another set of hooves, crashing against the ground. For a moment I thought my ears were playing tricks, but as the seconds flashed by I got more and more sure that I was hearing something besides Thunder's own hooves, banging through the thorns and the weeds.

A few seconds later I realized what it was.

CHAPTER 6

Somehow, Seth Farnum had got a set of reins on Lightning and was slowly gaining on us. I twisted my neck as far toward the left as it would go. Even so I could barely see him, but it was enough to make my little heart sing again. Lightning didn't have a saddle on but it didn't seem to make any difference to Seth.

"Dellie!" he yelled. "Hang on! Don't let loose! Just hang on!" As if I had any other options.

It probably took another two or three minutes for Lightning to catch up, and then to push her way past Thunder on the left side so that Seth himself was pretty much even with my horse's head. At that point he reached down with his right hand and tried to snatch up Thunder's reins. But he missed, and Thunder just stretched his neck out even farther and went into overdrive. At the same time he turned slightly to the left. We were very close to the forest by then, so that move—seemingly random but away from the bushes and the trees—was probably another lifesaver for both of us.

Lightning had to bend to the left, too, but that didn't slow her down. Somehow she pushed her way past Thunder once more. And this time, when Seth reached down for the reins he got both of them at once.

Immediately he pulled back on them as straight along Thunder's side as he could, which pulled the horse's head back a tiny bit with his nose angled to the left. Seth yelled at me at the same time: "Hang on, Dellie! I'll try to slow him down and stop him!"

At first I wasn't sure he could do it, especially since he was riding bareback and had no stirrups and no saddle horn to help hold him on. Fortunately, as Joey Falcon's father explained later, Lightning had been trained as a stock horse so she knew enough to hold her position exactly where Seth had put her. She matched Thunder stride-for-stride, even as both horses continued to race full speed ahead. I have no idea how they managed to keep their legs from tangling up together.

And then things started changing a tiny little bit. It wasn't much at first, but gradually

Thunder began responding to the pull of the reins against the bit in his mouth, slowing his frantic pace down little by little. At the same time, the more he gave in to the pressure the more Seth was able to increase it, until at last Thunder slowed to a walk and then came to a total stop.

By then he was covered in sweat and blowing like a steam engine. I didn't have enough breath left to blow anything at all, and my pants and shirt were soaking wet where they'd been pressed up against Thunder's body. But both horses were stopped, and Seth and I instantly jumped down. For the first time, Seth handed Thunder's reins to me.

"Let's let them cool down a minute and then we can walk them back," he said. I was in total agreement. My arms and legs were so cramped, from all the desperate hanging on, that I didn't even want to think about riding all the way back to the others. And I was still out of breath myself, although I was starting to get it back.

"Thank you!" I finally said. "Thank you, Seth! I couldn't do anything to stop him. You probably saved my life!"

Seth lowered his head and nodded it very slightly. "Just glad it ended," he said. "Could have been bad. Glad we got you stopped."

I wanted to hug him but I couldn't have reached above his waist. And I didn't think he would have understood. So I simply nodded my own head a half-dozen times. I wanted to smile but I couldn't get my mouth to cooperate.

"That was scary," I finally said. "That was really scary! If you hadn't stopped him I think I would have landed on a stone or a tree at some point!"

Seth didn't say anything for another minute or so, but finally he looked at me sideways and motioned toward Thunder. "Let's see if we can walk them back. I think they're both ready. Just lead him with the reins but don't pull too hard. We don't want to lose him again after all this."

We had no easy way to get over the fence on foot, so we had to walk over to a gate maybe fifty yards away from where we'd both crossed a few minutes earlier. I don't think it had been used very much so it wasn't too keen on opening up, but we finally got it.

You can probably imagine how everyone cheered when Seth and I got back to where the crowd was waiting. Two or three of the guys had run out to help us bring the horses along, and they had big smiles too. Joey and his father immediately took charge of Thunder and Lightning and started toweling and brushing them down.

"I think that's enough riding for one day," said Joey's mother, once she'd made sure I wasn't really hurt. She must have come out of the house when all the fun started. Something in the way she looked at all of us told me this wasn't the first near-calamity she'd seen.

Before long, lunch was ready and things soon got back to normal.

The very next day was Sunday. I was still feeling a little pain in my legs and I wasn't sure I wanted to walk to the church for Sunday School, but Cake Baker showed up right on time and wouldn't even let me think about staying home.

"Dellie, you have to go! Everybody in the place will want to see you and Seth, to make sure you're all right and listen to your story all over again!"

"Why would they want to listen?" I said. "They were there and they saw it for themselves."

She gave me one of her looks and I knew enough to shut up. Cake Baker was not somebody you could argue with. Besides, a secret part of me probably wanted to revel in the attention I knew Seth and I would get.

Sadly, though, when we got there Seth wasn't anywhere around, and he never showed up. But that didn't stop Mr. Morgan—who was both our Sunday School teacher on Sunday morning and our youth group leader on Tuesday night—from turning the whole thing into a huge object lesson.

"Based on what I've been hearing," he began, "I really missed something yesterday. Something not only exciting, but something that I think might have shown some of you a side of one of your new friends that you hadn't seen before! Anybody want to comment on that?"

I never did find out why Mr. Morgan hadn't been there the day before, but I knew he sometimes had medical emergencies that pulled him away from things at the last minute. Even so he seemed to know a little bit about what had happened, even if he didn't yet have all the details. He was also an expert at opening up a subject without ever taking a position of his own—or owning up to what he knew—until he absolutely had to. This was no exception.

Joey Falcon finally raised his hand. "Well, it was my house and my horses so I guess I ought to at least explain what all the fuss is about." He paused, looked around at the others, then continued. "If you were there you saw Seth Farnum go out and catch a horse named Thunder. We can't usually get a halter on without chasing him all over the place. But Seth caught him and brought him right in. Then, a few minutes later you saw that same horse get spooked and take off like a screaming banshee, with Dellie O'Shea in the saddle but without the reins in his hand yet. That's when Seth threw a bridle on Lightning, our other horse, and took off after Thunder."

People were nodding so Joey kept talking. "They both had to jump one of our fences, which is quite a mean trick all by itself. But Dellie stayed in the saddle, and even though Seth was riding bareback he eventually caught up and grabbed Thunder's reins. That let him stop Thunder from running away anymore, and everything got back to normal."

Joey's version wasn't exactly perfect but it gave Mr. Morgan the opening he needed. "My question," he said, after waiting in case someone else wanted to jump in, "is what do you think about a guy who can catch horses that nobody else can lay a glove on? What about how he caught up with Dellie and stopped the runaway? Couldn't Dellie have been hurt pretty bad if Seth hadn't helped him out?"

Nobody said a word for quite a little while. Finally Cake raised her hand. "I have to wonder if maybe we might have misjudged Seth—at least a little bit," she finally said. "There's a lot more to him than what we saw at first."

Again, nobody said a word for a while until Mr. Morgan jumped in again. "I don't know if we need to use the word 'misjudge,'" he said. "That could be a little harsh. I wonder if maybe some of us simply didn't understand what it can be like to come into a new group and not know for sure how to fit in. Would that be another way to say it?"

Along with everything else, Mr. Morgan had a gift for slapping his finger on things without tossing a whole bunch of blame around. By that time he had most of the kids in the room nodding their heads.

"That's probably the biggest point," said Hank, at last. "Seth doesn't talk much but he sure knows what to do when things go bad!"

"Yeah, and he might not look you in the eye but he knows how to look inside the mind of a horse."

"And how to deal with what he sees in there."

By then the comments were coming so fast and furious I had trouble getting recognized when I raised my hand. "From my point of view," I said as soon as I had a chance, "I don't care if he doesn't talk 'normal' to me for the rest of my life. The fact that I *have* a 'rest of my life' says it all!"

I hadn't intended to shut people down, but that's pretty much what happened at that point. Mr. Morgan smiled, sat there and waited for another thirty seconds, then finally took charge again.

"That really does say it all, Dellie," he said in his lowest and slowest voice. "So—why don't we open our lesson books and see what we're supposed to be discussing today? I think you'll find that it goes along very well with what we talked about a few days ago."

Which we all agreed with when we looked at that week's lesson. Turns out it was based on Proverbs 24:29.

Some things you just can't get away from.

CHAPTER 8

Things moved along fairly normal for the next two or three weeks. I saw Seth Farnum at school every day, and it was clear that our relationship had got a lot tighter than before. On the other hand, I can't say that we became best friends even though I will always be grateful to him for saving my bacon. But Seth just wasn't a "best buddy" kind of a guy. Over the years we had lots of short conversations, but he still looked sideways most of the time and almost never arranged his words in complete sentences. Many times it still seemed like talking to a zombie with a mouth that moved sideways.

Even so, almost like he was purposely responding to the other kids' secret questions about whether he was "normal" or not, he continued to show us things about himself that didn't make sense from where we were looking. One time that I especially remember, he came by the field next to my house where a bunch of us were playing baseball. Somehow or other he got put on one of the teams and wound up in right field—probably where they figured he couldn't do too much damage. But the other team had some leftie batters, and about halfway through the game one of them hit a long fly ball that was so far over Seth's head he had no chance whatsoever to catch up with it. Especially since it kept rolling halfway to forever once it hit the ground.

Meanwhile, one of our fastest runners was on first base. The minute he took off, everybody knew for sure that he'd score. And, even that the guy who'd hit the ball might have a home run as well. But Seth didn't give up. He chased the ball full speed, and when he finally caught up with it he whirled around, took two running steps toward the infield, then fired a perfect strike to the guy covering home plate.

Now, I don't know how much baseball you've played so let me explain something. Even the best fielders usually can't throw from the outer edges of the outfield all the way to home plate without at least one bounce. Or, they throw to one of the infielders and he relays it the rest of the way. Which, of course, takes more time.

But Seth didn't do that. He threw that ball on a straight line, for a distance way farther than the rest of us could equal. And the first runner, who'd already rounded third and had about ten feet yet to go, never had a chance. He didn't even slide because there was no point. He got tagged standing up, almost before he knew what was happening. Then he whirled around to see who'd thrown the ball like that!

When Seth came in at the end of the inning he made it seem like no big deal. To the rest of us it was the biggest "Wow!" of the day. On the other hand, Seth struck out three times and then popped up the only time he got a bat on the ball. Figure that one out.

But that stuff was only one small part of the whole story. Seth had one more unique talent that will take a bit of telling to cover so you'll understand. It all started one day when the weekly newspaper began hitting front porches around town. The very first page had a story about a seven-year-old girl named Ellie Peterson, who'd gone missing. Apparently her parents had contacted the paper an hour or two before they went to press that day, so the story was about as fresh as they got. No pictures in that era, unfortunately, but in a town of that size they really weren't so important. Everybody knew her parents even if they didn't know the girl.

I remember how the whole town got involved. About halfway through the school day the principle even came around and dismissed every single class. The idea was that we'd all go out and help the searchers comb the hills and valleys and ditches and wells, both in the town and on the outer edges. Which most of us did. But by nightfall of that first day, nobody had found a single clue. Eventually, most everybody went home—we didn't have flashlights yet, and burning torches and candles don't really help much when you're trying to find tiny little footprints in grass and weeds.

But things were about to change. Next morning, not long after first light, Cake Baker and I and a lot of other folks were out there again. Cake and I were trudging through another inch-by-inch look at one of the rock outcroppings on the edge of town when Seth Farnum suddenly appeared out of nowhere. He was shaking his head, hard.

"Not going to work," he said. "Not going to work. Not here. I go find her myself. Go by myself."

"Wait a minute, Seth!" I was almost shouting. "What do you mean? How do you know where Ellie is?"

"Don't know," he said. "Didn't say I knew, exactly. But she's not here. Much farther, out in the woods."

At that point he turned and began walking fast toward the trees not far from the edge of town—where the runaway horse had almost taken me not too long ago. This was one of the thickest forests I've ever seen, and by most accounts it went on for miles and miles. Very few people ever ventured too far inside. On the outside edges the briars and the other bushes filled up most of the spaces between the trees. Once you got fifty yards or so inside, the tops of the trees blocked most of the sun so that not much short stuff grew on the ground. This made it easier to walk between the trees, but also made it harder and harder to tell where you were.

"Wait!" This time I actually did shout. "Wait! If you're going in there you can't do it alone. Give me a minute—let's get some others to go with you."

Seth hesitated, and Cake and I immediately climbed down from the rocks. "There's Ellie's father over there," she said, pointing to a taller man with a wide-brimmed hat and what we now might call "hiking boots" on his feet. He was talking to several other men, and gesturing all over the place. "Stay right there, Seth! Let us talk to him!"

It didn't take us long to explain what Seth wanted to do. Mr. Peterson didn't seem much interested at first. Clearly he was more than a little shook up, yet I don't think he was convinced that his daughter could have gone very far beyond the town itself. But Ellie had been missing for a full day-and-a-half by then, and he was getting desperate. He looked back and forth at Seth, Cake, and me for a full minute or so before he finally nodded his head, ever so slightly.

"All right. Let's try it." He said it so quietly I almost couldn't hear, but Seth must have read his lips because he started moving toward us.

"We need to go now," he said. "We need to go now."

"All right, son—just give us a minute. Let's make sure we have a good compass. Once we get in there we're going to need it. And maybe some other things, too. I don't want to risk any more lives by getting careless and doing something stupid."

CHAPTER 9

I'm not sure how Ellie's father convinced them, but it didn't take him long to form up a group of about five other men, plus Seth and Cake and me. Seth then had to wait for one of the guys to run back to his house and grab a compass, along with one or two other things that were stuffed into a couple of primitive-looking backpacks. I remember hoping there'd be some food in there, too, but I didn't want to ask. By the time everybody was ready Seth was having trouble keeping his cool.

"We have to go! We have to go!" He said it over and over, each time a little louder with a little more worry shadowing his face. But pretty soon we got underway, with Seth in the lead. He headed straight into the woods. Then, after we'd slogged our way through the underbrush around the outer edge he stopped and acted like he was listening for something. When he started up again he took a slightly different route, more toward the west than anything else. At least, that was my impression—I wasn't the one with the compass so I could only go by instinct.

We hadn't been moving through the trees very long when we ran into our first problem. The land itself was like a wild jungle, with hills and valleys, huge rocks, wide swales that bordered on mini-swamps, and all kinds of other land formations folding into each other. If we could've seen the whole thing on a topographical map I'm sure it would have looked anything but flat.

After a half hour or so we came to the edge of a downgrade that didn't look especially steep. Yet the minute Cake and I stepped onto it, from the upper level, we both wound up sliding downhill on our backs. Fortunately—and unlike most girls of that age in that time and place—Cake Baker, the original tomboy, was wearing pants instead of a dress. Otherwise she could have ripped all the skin off her legs. As it was we both half-slid and half-tumbled down the slope until we finally came to a rest at the bottom, and neither one of us was feeling too good.

It took me a few seconds to find my voice. "Are you hurt? Myself, I think my body is now just a giant bruise."

"Me too," she said. "I think I know the first name of every rock from here to the top. But I don't think I broke anything or wrecked anything permanent."

By that time the others had joined us at the bottom and were pulling both of us to our feet. Somehow they'd all managed to stay upright on their own. Fortunately, Cake and I had apparently led the way in the direction Seth wanted to go. So once we knew we hadn't broken anything we kept moving forward, through the moss and the occasional muck between the trees.

Suddenly we began to hear the sound of running water, very faint at first but growing louder as we moved forward, until we found ourselves standing on a sandy, sloping bank beside the source of the noise. "I didn't know there was a river out here," said one of the men. But there was, although it really didn't seem like much more than a noisy stream. It might have been ten or twelve feet wide at the most. But it was moving fast enough to make quite a commotion when you got close.

"I think this feeds into the Calabas River," said Ellie's father. Then he added something else, almost as an afterthought. "If Ellie came this way I sure hope she didn't try to get across." Nobody said anything more. It didn't seem very deep, but I'm sure we all knew what he was thinking.

"We turn here," said Seth, who'd been rocking back and forth on his haunches, scanning the river and the trees beside it, all the while with one of his hands cupped around his ear. "We follow the water."

At that point he started walking again, along the upper edge of the bank. The river headed north at first and then slowly turned west in a wide arc, following what must have started out as a natural dip in the land. By now the trees appeared to be getting thicker and thicker, with an ever tighter canopy of leaves overhead that made the place seem darker and darker.

But Seth didn't seem to notice, and no one else was concentrating on anything except keeping the group together. Suddenly, without any explanation at all, Seth turned north again, away from the water. In five minutes we'd left the gurgle of the water far behind. The only sound became the crunch of our shoes on the ground, and the occasional swish of a low branch against us as we shouldered it aside.

I had to wonder what Ellie Peterson's father was thinking. Why was he so willing to follow a young man he'd probably never met before today? What possible proof could he have that Seth Farnum knew anything he didn't know himself? And then I realized that Cake and I were doing exactly the same thing. There wasn't any logic involved; nothing but hope balanced against what would have been despair . . . except that we all refused to admit it.

On we went, through the trees for at least another hour. By this time some of us were beginning to react to the blistering pace Seth had set from the beginning. But no one tried to slow it down, even though it was obvious to me that some of Mr. Peterson's friends, not all of whom were exactly "fit and trim," were feeling some pain. Suddenly, Seth Farnum stopped dead in his tracks and motioned for the rest of us to do the same.

One by one we then moved up behind him and looked where he pointed. Straight ahead, not more than twenty or thirty yards, we saw a small clearing in the trees where the soil appeared to be too heavily covered with rock to allow more tress to grow. On the other side were several dog-sized animals, milling around one of the trees right on the edge. I'd never seen any in the actual wild before, but it didn't take more than about three seconds to realize that we were looking at a small pack of wolves.

Meanwhile, probably twelve or fifteen feet off the ground, a little girl sat on one of the branches, her arms wrapped around the main trunk and her face turned the other way and tucked down almost to her shoulder.

"Oh my! I don't believe it!" said Mr. Peterson, so loud that the wolves stopped moving and pointed their heads in our direction, with their noses sniffing the air. Even then Mr. Peterson's "Oh my!" made him sound a lot more like a bald-headed banker finding a penny on the floor instead of a father finding his long-lost daughter. But that's how it went.

"Oh my! I think that's Ellie!"

MORE THAN ONE WAY TO SCARE A WOLF

CHAPTER 10

Seth Farnum didn't waste any time. "We have a gun?" He pointed straight ahead, as if we hadn't yet figured out what was going on. I think we all knew what we were seeing, but Mr. Peterson didn't act like it mattered.

"We didn't bring any guns. But all we have to do is charge over there and make a lot of noise. They'll scatter like leaves in the wind. I mean it—let's go!"

I'm not so sure that everyone else agreed, but this wasn't one of those situations that allow you to take a vote and make sure you're all on the same page before you make a move. I think we all knew that Mr. Peterson would go ripping across that clearing on his own if we didn't get on board. So we all took off at once.

Altogether there were only nine of us, but I think we made enough commotion for a hundred or so. Mr. Peterson tore out in front and probably screamed the loudest, but together we bellowed like banshees and waved enough arms to look and sound like the Roman Army chasing the British into the North Sea a couple thousand years earlier.

The wolves didn't stand a chance. They had no idea what was happening. Instantly they all lurched around and took off in the opposite direction. Within seconds we were standing under the tree. And now it was the little girl's turn to scream.

"Daddy! Daddy! Daddy! I can't believe it! It's Daddy!"

In a matter of about four seconds she swung herself around, wrapped her legs around the trunk, and slid down the tree. I'm not sure what kind it was, but the bark was smooth. So smooth, in fact, that she dropped into her father's arms at the speed of light—so fast that she landed almost before he got ready.

I remember wondering how she'd got up there in the first place. But this wasn't the time to worry about that. Everyone in the crowd had tears in his or her eyes by the time Ellie's father finally found his own voice.

"Oh Ellie! Thank God we found you! How did you ever get so far away? What in the world were you thinking of?"

Ellie didn't say a word for almost a full

minute. Just wrapped her arms around her father's neck and held on tight, with tears running down her cheeks. Finally she pulled far enough away to look him in the eye.

"I don't know, Daddy! I don't know! I just went for a walk and followed a butterfly through the bushes. I almost caught him, too! And then, I looked around me and I was lost. I tried to get back but I didn't know how to come home again. And then, when it started to get dark last night I heard some animals coming and climbed up the tree! I thought they would get me!"

They both tightened their grip around each other again. Only this time Ellie's father began to nod, as though he had begun to understand. "Oh Ellie, you did exactly the right thing. Mommy and I wish you hadn't wandered off, but you did everything else exactly right. You did the smartest thing you could possibly do!"

Once again she loosened her arms from his neck, pulled slightly away, and began scanning the ground. "Daddy! Where are the foxes now? What if they come back?"

He almost smiled before he corrected her. "Those weren't foxes, honey. Those were wolves! But don't worry about that now.

They're not coming back. And if they do we've got lots of ways to protect you. It's all over now. You're safe." And then he hugged her one more time.

It was obvious from her torn clothes and the red scratches on her arms and legs that little Ellie had been through some rough country. I thought back to the brambles and other low-lying bushes at the edge of the forest and couldn't help flinching a little myself. All the rest of us had pants and long sleeves on.

By that point Cake Baker couldn't resist stroking Ellie's hair and murmuring a few words to her. "We'll get you home, sweetheart. You don't have to worry anymore. We'll get you home so you can hug your mommy again, too!"

Ironically, the one person who seemed to be the least bit tuned-in to all this was the guy who led us there in the first place. I wasn't sure whether Seth was embarrassed or just caught in one more situation in which he somehow didn't know how to act. Now that he'd done the job he couldn't seem to keep his face upright and his eyes off the ground.

But Mr. Peterson was in no mood to notice. As soon as he could shift Ellie to his left arm he grabbed Seth by the shoulder and squeezed him so hard he almost cracked the poor guy's shoulder blade. Or so it appeared to me—I was close enough to see Seth wince.

"I don't know what to say to you, son. I really don't know what to say! I don't know how you were able to do it! But without you we could have lost our daughter. You saved her life, and maybe mine and her mother's as well. I'm not so sure we could have kept our own heads on straight if those wolves had got my little girl down from that tree!"

Seth actually smiled at that point, but only for a second. "We need go," he said, his face turning serious again. "We need go. Wolves come back—we don't want a fight. If you ready, let's go. And don't let anybody get behind."

All this in his usual halting voice, pointing back toward the way we'd come and taking several quick strides even as he spoke. Then he halted to made sure everyone was following him.

He needn't have worried. None of us wanted to be there another second, least of all Ellie Peterson and her father. He offered to get her something to eat from one of the backpacks, but I think she was too wrought up to think about food. Or even about water. So he swung her up onto his shoulders and that's where she rode, all the way back to town.

HOMECOMING

CHAPTER 11

It's probably not necessary to point out that we didn't need the compass on the way home. Even if we hadn't had one with us we would have been okay—a couple of the men had marked our trail as we moved along, so it was easy to find our way back to the river we'd followed earlier.

Even so, Seth took the lead again and set a ferocious pace. From there it was simply a matter of following the river back to the bend where it had turned west, then south to the point where we'd come upon it an hour or two earlier. But no matter how obvious things might have been, I don't think Seth had any intention of trusting any instincts except his own. He stayed out in front all the way, and when we came to the place where we'd first met up with the river he made the final turn back toward town before the rest of us even realized we'd arrived.

This time Cake and I managed to stay on our feet as we climbed back up the hill we'd slid down before. An hour or so later we came to the edge of the forest, fought our way through the bushes, and emerged just beyond the field in which Joey Falcon's two horses were grazing in utter contentment.

In a few more minutes we'd gone through the gates on Joey's property and walked back into town. Along the way, some of the people who were still out searching the area began to recognize us. Or, at the very least, they must have recognized Mr. Peterson, who was still carrying Ellie on his shoulders with her legs hanging down on either side. By the time we'd gone a few blocks toward the Peterson house we'd picked up at least a couple dozen stragglers, all delighted to see that we'd found his little daughter.

Without doubt the best reception we got came when Ellie's mother slammed open the door, tore out of the house, and pulled her daughter right off her husband's neck. She must have seen us coming through the window. I can't remember what she said, but that's partly because I couldn't make most of it out. I'm not even sure she was speaking actual words. Mostly, it was all hugs, tears, big wet smooches, and then more of the same. If she had anything negative to say, by way of teaching Ellie not to go wandering off anymore, she saved it for later.

At last, just before the family went inside to be alone with their daughter and their other kids, Mr. Peterson turned to all of us who'd gone into the forest with him and thanked every single one. When he got to Seth Farnum again I almost didn't think he was going to let go of Seth's hand. He grabbed it with both of his own, at which point his emotions really choked him up, to the point where he simply could not talk except for the same two words. I know he said "Thank you!" over and over, until Seth himself was looking so embarrassed I thought he might melt down into a greasy blob and disappear.

The only other words I remember from that reunion came just before we all went home. Mrs. Peterson leaned over to her husband, as they were heading into their house. "Did you really carry Ellie all the way back by yourself? You're gonna' need some kind of work on your neck tonight or you won't be able to move your head tomorrow! She's really not that little anymore, you know?"

"She's not heavy; she's my daughter," he said. I'm not sure whether the folks who turned that line into "He's not heavy—he's my brother" many years later actually stole it from Ellie's father. But I am sure that God can give the right words to anyone He wants, anytime He wants.

Along with a lot of other things, too.

GOLDEN REFLECTIONS AND GOLDEN FEELINGS

CHAPTER 12

The next Tuesday came about four days later. As usual, Cake Baker came over to my place after supper so we could walk over to the Morgans' house together. But this time things weren't quite the same. She had someone else with her. Seth Farnum had figured out how to join the club.

I think everybody knew in advance that the main subject for that evening would be the rescue of Ellie Peterson, with all its implications. Mr. Morgan didn't disappoint us. After a few of the usual comments on things that were going on in the lives of the other kids, he got right into the latest news.

"How many know about the little girl who got lost? Her name is Ellie Peterson. Some of you were there when she was found. Who knows that story?"

Just about every right hand in the room went up, with the exception of Joey Falcon's. I don't remember why but his right arm was in a cast, hanging from a sling, which Mr.

Morgan had asked him about earlier. So he stuck his left hand up instead. And he's the one Mr. Morgan pointed at.

"What about it, Joey?"

"Well, we all got word that Ellie Peterson was missing. So we all left school and helped look for her. But she wasn't anywhere around. No tracks that anybody could be sure were hers, and nothing else to go on."

"All right—what happened next?"

"Well, I wasn't close enough to actually see it happen but they tell me that eventually Seth Farnum came along and acted like he knew where she was. I don't think he really did, but somehow he seemed to know where to look."

Mr. Morgan looked around the room until he spotted Cake Baker. "Paisley, didn't you and Dellie go with Seth? What happened?"

Cake Baker looked at me, and for a moment I thought she was going to make me do the talking instead. But I was wrong. "I don't have any idea what Seth knew or how he knew it," she said. "But he did seem to have some 'special knowledge' that nobody else had. Somehow he knew which way to go, and in the end he led us straight into the woods to where Ellie was."

She stopped and looked at Seth with a big smile on her face. By that time he looked like he'd rather be anywhere else in the world. He'd aimed his face toward the floor and hunched his shoulders up so they were higher than his neck. But since he was sitting beside me I could also sense enough of what was going on to suspect that he was smiling. If not on the outside, certainly somewhere else. Otherwise he would have had to be made out of stone.

Mr. Morgan's voice softened noticeably when he spoke directly to the real hero of the day. "How did you know, Seth? Did you just feel it, or did you really, absolutely know, like you'd know your own name?"

"Can't say," Seth said after a long pause. "Don't know. Just did what felt right. Felt right to me. Don't know how or why, but something told me she'd gone in the woods. And when we got there I just followed . . . just followed . . . I don't really know what."

Eric Topper jumped in at that point. He was clearly frustrated. "Can't you explain it a little better than that? We really want to know!"

"Don't do words!" Suddenly Seth was almost shouting. "Don't do words! Do *things*!

Words float away—things stay! Things are real!"

That shut everybody up for several seconds. Finally Mr. Morgan got back in the game. "Seth, I think I understand what you're saying. To me, what you're talking about sounds like either instinct or inspiration. And either way, it also sounds like something God Himself is involved in."

Eric Topper couldn't resist. "So, if that's true, does God talk to you in your head or do you just feel it in your bones?"

"God not in my head! God in my heart!"

Once again everybody shut up. You could almost feel the tension in the room, not from conflict but from the sudden, unexpected implication—and the powerful truth—of what Seth had said. Then Mr. Morgan pulled his chair over and put his hand on Seth's shoulder. And for the first time since I'd known him, Seth didn't object.

"God bless you, Seth. God bless you! There's no finer place for Him than in your heart!"

At that point some kind of dam must have broken inside Seth. I don't think he was crying but his voice got even more broken up than usual. "God in my heart a long time. I asked Him . . . long time ago. But He still hasn't made me like everybody else! I try to be but I can't! I can't talk fast or fancy. I can't focus my looking like other people do. And I can't . . . I can't . . . "

By then his head was in his hands, but he still wasn't crying. At least, not out loud. Mr. Morgan moved his arm and put it all the way around Seth's shoulders. But he knew enough to simply sit there and not try to talk. Then Cake Baker—who definitely *was* tearing up—walked over and did the same. That seemed like the signal for everyone else to gather around, and for the next five minutes the whole group stood in a circle around Seth. No one said a word. Most of the kids had their heads bowed. Finally, Seth raised his own and tried to talk again.

"Not mad at God. Don't want to make you think that. I'm glad to be me! Glad He cares about me! Glad He loves me! But I'm not always as much like Him as I'd like to be."

I suspect that even Mr. Morgan was ready to whimper by then. But he still had enough sense not to try to talk, or to do anything else to put Seth Farnum any more on the spot.

He simply stood up, moved his chair back into the circle, and sat down. One by one the others returned to their seats too. And still, nobody said a word until most of the bowed heads came back up. I don't think I've ever seen so many happy faces in such a small space.

Mr. Morgan waited until exactly the right moment before he nodded his head several times. Then he looked directly at the main focus of all that caring.

"Seth, it's an honor to have you with us. And no, you don't need to worry about changing or being someone else. Not here, not in front of God, and certainly not in front of us. You just be the person God made you and we'll all keep on being proud of you."

He looked around the room one final time. "Now, unless anyone else has something they need to say, I think we've done enough for tonight."

And that's the way Seth Farnum came into town and saved two lives. He also became an honored member of our group. But I guess you already know that.

FINAL THOUGHTS

CHAPTER 13

As I've said in other books, Cake Baker and I never got romantic. But we remained good friends long after she married someone else. Even after I left New Hampshire for St. Louis when I was in my early 20s, we were still long-distance buddies. Can't explain why, but somehow she and I were in better synch than I've ever been with anyone else, with the possible exception of a guy I met later on, named Patrick Allen. And, of course, my own wife, tiny little Lorelei. But we can't get into that story here!

Meanwhile, I knew Seth Farnum for several more years after the Ellie rescue, but I never saw him change very much. Nowadays we know almost for sure that Seth was autistic. And once autistic, always autistic, I guess. He certainly never turned into a social butterfly. But somewhere along the line, when he was still in high school, of all things he got his hands on some diamond-cutting equipment and began trimming and polishing diamonds.

I'm not sure how he got his training. But one thing I did learn about Seth. He might not have been much of a conversation builder but he read a lot of books. I'm sure there must have been some books on diamond cutting out there somewhere. Our town didn't have a big library, but Seth knew they could borrow books from the bigger ones in the bigger cities. Cake Baker worked in the local one; she told me he kept a lot of volumes moving back and forth. By the time we got into high school I don't think I ever saw him without a book in his hand. And most of the time they didn't seem to be textbooks, either.

He also seemed to have an unusual eye for beauty—for the way things looked. If he'd been born fifty years later he might have been a movie maker. He used to look out the window and frame whatever he saw with his hands, like movie people do nowadays. Or, like ordinary people sometimes do if they want to make whoever's watching think they're seeing something special. But I don't think Seth Farnum had any false bones like that in his entire body. He simply wasn't able to be a deceiver.

To be a diamond cutter, of course, he also had to figure out where and how to buy pieces of what they call "rough," which are uncut lumps of diamond that look more like milky glass before they're turned into finished gemstones. It occurs to me that Seth himself was somewhat like a rough diamond for most of his life. But there were also times when he seemed about as polished and refined as anyone can possibly be.

It's hard to shine much brighter than when you're saving somebody's life.

Appendix 1
How to Create Golden Turnabouts in Your Own Life

(1) Why do you think people call it the "golden rule"? What is there about it that's "golden"?

_____

_____

_____

_____

(2) If you had to rewrite the golden rule in your own words, how would you say it?

_____

_____

_____

_____

(3) Why do you think Seth Farnum objected so hard when Dellie touched him on the shoulder? Was it a physical reason, a mental reason—or both? Explain.

_____

_____

_____

_____

(4) What things do you think Seth Farnum must have understood, even if he couldn't put them into words, when he brought in the horse that no one else could catch? (Hint: There are at least two concepts at work here!)

_____

_____

_____

_____

_____

(5) Why do you think Thunder, the black horse, ran away with Dellie on his back? Whose fault was it?

_____

_____

_____

_____

_____

(6) Everyone seems to agree that what Seth Farnum did to save Dellie's life took lots of courage. But why? What could have happened instead of what _did_ happen?

_____

_____

_____

_____

_____

(7) Are you familiar with the word "autistic"? What does it mean?

_____

_____

_____

_____

_____

(8) Why do you suppose that many autistic people have other "gifts" that most people don't have? Does God sometimes try to balance things out that way, or do some "gifts" come about because of other causes that are purely physical or emotional?

_____

_____

_____

_____

_____

(9) How do you think Seth Farnum knew where Ellie had gone?

_____

_____

_____

_____

_____

(10) Why did the wolves run away when the men made noise and ran toward them? Was that a safe thing to do? Why did the wolves not come back and attack them later?

_____

_____

_____

_____

_____

(11) Why did Mr. Peterson carry his daughter all the way home? Wouldn't that have been very tiring?

_____

_____

_____

_____

_____

(12) Have you ever seen anyone else act according to the golden rule? Describe how it happened and how it turned out.

_____

_____

_____

_____

_____

_____

Appendix 2
How to Apply the Golden Rule in Your Own Life

With Your Parents
- Treat them with respect at all times.
- Listen to what they say, and act accordingly.
- Ask for their help in planning your future. Don't be a lone wolf.

With Your Brothers or Sisters
- Avoid arguments and other disagreements.
- Be kind to them any way you can.
- Offer to help the younger ones learn new things.

With Your Friends at School
- No cheating, whether others are watching you or not.
- Don't hesitate to ask for help when you need it.
- Share your knowledge and understanding with those who need *your* help.

With Your Friends at Church
- Be patient. Help them learn biblical truths.
- Don't be too quick to judge them. Let God deal with their hearts.
- Be willing to talk about your own relationship with Him.

With Other People on Sports Teams, in Games, or in Practice
- Play fair. Follow the rules, whether they're written or unspoken.
- Never make fun of another player's performance.
- Don't try to do too much by yourself. Be a team player instead.

With Others at Your Place of Work
- Know what your boss expects. Ask if you're not sure.
- Always give an honest effort.
- Don't hesitate to ask for help, or to offer help if others need it.

With All Other People
- Be as friendly as the situation allows.
- Never take people for granted. Ask if you're not sure what they need or want.
- Dress and act in appropriate ways at all times.

Appendix 3
Where did the Golden Rule Actually Come From?

If you've read the complete *Dellie O'Shea*, which is the story of a major part of my adult life as a midget ragtime entertainer, you might remember my friend Jamie Goldstein. Jamie also shows up in some of these earlier stories, although I was so used to having him around I didn't always say much about him.

Jamie came from a Jewish family, and somewhere along the line I mentioned to him that we'd studied the golden rule a few days before Seth Farnum saved my life. And the day after too, although it came from a different place in the Bible the second time we studied it.

But when I quoted it to him from the New Testament, as clear as I could remember it, he immediately held up his hand. "That wasn't original with him," he said. "Jesus Christ was not the first person to say that."

"Then who did?"

"Well, I can think of two answers. There's a verse in Proverbs that says almost the same thing. Whether Solomon wrote it I don't know for sure, but it was certainly the same idea.

"But it was also taught by one of our own ancient teachers, very famous among my people. They called him Hillel the Elder, and if I remember correctly here's what he said:

"That which is despicable to you, do not do to your fellow. This is the whole Torah and the rest is commentary. Go and learn it.

"Hillel said it first, then probably taught it to another teacher named Gamaliel, who then taught it to that other guy in your New Testament, called Paul. And by 'Torah,' of course, he meant the first five books of the Old Testament.

"But that's not the point. Even though my own people don't accept him as their Messiah, Jesus Christ was still a Jew. But I think Hillel might have passed away too soon to teach it to him directly. So, He probably heard it from the teachers in the Temple."

I was amazed at how much Jamie knew about the Bible, including the New Testament. I couldn't possibly argue with any of it. Besides, it didn't really matter. Seth Farnum never asked where the basic impulse came from when he jumped on that other horse and took off after me. Likewise when he led the rest of us into the woods and found Ellie Peterson.

Some things just rise above all our "human" understanding.

Appendix 4
A Word About Autism

Near the end of the 19th century, in approximately 1897 when I was twelve years old and was actually living through the story in this book, the word "autism" hadn't been coined yet. That didn't happen until 1943, when a man named Leo Kanner used it in an article he wrote for a scientific journal called *Nervous Child*. However, Kanner actually borrowed the term from a German word, "autismus," which was first used by a Swiss psychiatrist named Eugen Bleuler. Bleuler passed away in 1950.

In any case, if there's one single point I hope you'll take away from everything I've written in this book, as Mr. Morgan also explained, *autism is not a disease*. It is nothing more than a minor, non-threatening condition in which the person's brain does not always work quite the same way as others. In scientific terms, autism is known as a *neural* condition. Some of the millions of cells in the brain, called *neurons*, do not process and transmit information quite as easily, as completely, or as productively as they might.

Typically, autistic people tend to be less socially adept than others. So, they sometimes have trouble carrying on normal conversations. At other times they may tend to act in a repetitive manner—for example, they might seem to be doing the same thing over and over again, for no apparent reason. However, they do not tend to be aggressive and are often quite likable people—just somewhat "different" than the average person.

Autism has been with us for a long time. But those who study such things tell us that it seems to be occurring more often in the modern age. On the other hand, part of that impression might come from our greater ability to detect it. And because, at least here in America, we tend to be a more heavily populated society. We now tend to live closer, and to interact more often, with more people than we might have done some sixty years ago, when I was a young man.

Note from the publisher: *You might be reading the above words in 2012 or later, but Dellie O'Shea wrote them more than 50 years ago, around 1960. A lot of what he said was especially "prescient," meaning that he seemed to be looking ahead with uncommon foresight and* *talking about how certain things would turn out in later years. Everything he said about autism is even more true today.*

However, we took the liberty of inserting slightly more modern versions of the biblical quotations Dellie wanted at the very beginning of this book. We kept the actual quotes that Dellie and his friends used within the text itself, along with an explanation of why they were using the King James Version of the Bible. But it made sense to us to use more familiar biblical language in the introductory pages.

Finally, one more thing that Dellie wouldn't have known much about. The instinctive method that Seth Farnum used to catch those two horses, Thunder and Lightning, has now been certified as correct by many of the modern horse experts, even though a lot of cowboys still don't use it. In modern equestrian language it's called the "Pressure and Release Method." A variation of that approach is also used, nowadays, to train horses to carry a rider. Horses don't need to be "broken." They need to be given the opportunity to cooperate with riders who understand how to be partners with them.

In that sense they can be a little bit like people. Horses are probably not autistic, but sometimes they operate in some of the same ways.

Other resources available from
The 1687 Foundation

31 Days of Praise
by Ruth Myers
also available in Spanish.

Christians who long to experience God in a fresh, deeper way will treasure this powerful, personal praise guide. Every day for just one month, a Scripture-based devotion cultivates the "heart habit" of praise and worship. Readers will be amazed to discover how their lives can be *touched* and *changed* on a day-by-day, month-by-month basis. They will be gently inspired to appreciate and adore the Lord in all things—yes, even in the midst of pain, disappointment, and heartache. A deeper intim acy with God, and a greater love for Him, is the sure result. Come into His presence with praise.

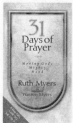

31 Days of Prayer
by Ruth Myers
also available in Spanish.

God invites us—*welcomes us*—into the high privilege of talking and working with Him. *31 Days of Prayer* shows you how to enjoy that privilege and begin an incredible prayer adventure. You'll discover in new ways that prayer is the slender nerve that moves the mighty hand of God. This is the perfect book to lead you in prayer for a full month—or many months—and help you create a prayer habit that lasts a lifetime. Rise above earthbound living…and into a new awareness of the Lord's delightful presence!

Karla Faye Tucker Set Free:
Life and Faith on Death Row
by Linda Strom

Karla Faye Tucker, the first woman executed in Texas in over one hundred years, became an evangelist for Christ during her fourteen-year imprisonment on Death Row. This is the story of Karla's spiritual journey, the women and men she reached, and the God who offers redemption and hope to the hardest of hearts.

Fruit Happens!
by Michael Christopher

Fruit happens when you spend time with God! *Fruit Happens!* also features one of the most exciting characters you might ever meet. His name is Dellie O'Shea, and his game is "over the top" in every possible way.

Dellie O'Shea is not someone who sits on the sidelines and watches the world pass by. He's a young man who puts his best instincts into action, especially those he gets directly from God. Along the way he learns what the "Fruits of the Spirit" are all about, by saving the life of another even as those same spiritual fruits grow and develop within himself.

He's also a Very Special Person in other ways as well—but you'll have to read his story to find out what they are!

Golden Turnabout
by Michael Christopher

Golden Turnabouts happen when you see with more than your eyes!

Golden Turnabout is the second in a series, featuring most of the same fascinating characters you've met before—including Dellie O'Shea! This time Dellie makes a new friend who seems to be slightly different from anyone else he's ever known. And maybe a little more prickly, too.

But things aren't always the way they first appear. Sometimes we judge a little too quickly, based on what we see on the outside before we have a chance to look a little deeper. And sometimes when we least expect it, others "do unto us" in ways that change our world for the better, even as Christ Himself would have us "do unto them."

Psalm 91: God's Umbrella of Protection
by Peggy Joyce Ruth
also available in Spanish.

Do the latest statistics on cancer, heart disease, and other medical conditions send a chill down your spine? Do thoughts of terrorist attacks and chemical warfare cause your heart to skip a beat? What about all the natural disasters that strike in unexpected places? Indeed—do you sometimes wonder if there is any safe haven anywhere in the world in which you might someday want to hide? If any of these things have ever troubled you, this can be one of the most important books you will ever read! In Psalm 91, the author's highly revealing, biblically based examination of the blessings God promises will open your heart, strengthen your spirit, and revitalize every aspect of your life!

Psalm 91:
God's Shield of Protection
(Military Edition)
by Peggy Joyce Ruth
and Angelia Ruth Schum

Everything that's true about the "regular" edition of this book is also true of the Military Edition—only *more* so! This version is filled with military applications—almost every story has a military slant, and every testimonial comes from someone in the military who has *seen the God of Psalm 91 in action* in military situations, including combat. Many of these testimonials will astound and amaze you—God steps in again and again to protect His people and keep His promises. No situation is hopeless when God is in charge. This book proves it over and over again.

My Own Psalm 91
by Peggy Joyce Ruth
also available in Spanish

The Cross Pin
(shown mounted on card)

To request books or cross pins,
or for more information, please contact:
The 1687 Foundation
P.O. Box 1961
Sisters, OR 97759
Email: info@1687foundation.com
541.549.7600 tel
541.549.7603 fax